THE STAR WARS TRILOGY SCRAPBOOK
THE REBEL ALLIANCE

by Mark Cotta Vaz

SCHOLASTIC INC.

New York   Toronto   London   Auckland   Sydney

With love to the Augustino clan, especially Sue, Harley, and Carson; and loving thoughts to Jim Augustino—at one with the Force!

ACKNOWLEDGEMENTS

Many thanks to all the Lucasfilm folks, including publishing head Lucy Autrey Wilson and editor Jane Mason (and may the Force be with Lucasfilmers Tina Mills and Cara Evangelista as well). On the Scholastic side, my appreciation to editors Jennifer Johnson and Susan Kitzen.

ISBN 0-590-12051-4

TM & ® & © 1997 Lucasfilm Ltd.
All rights reserved. Published by Scholastic Inc.

Book design by Todd Lefelt

12 11 10 9 8 7 6 5 4 3 2 1   7 8 9/9 0 1 2/0

Printed in the U.S.A.

First Scholastic printing, November 1997

CONTENTS

INTRODUCTION:
THE LIGHT OF THE FORCE

It was a time of deadly trouble. The galaxy had enjoyed peace and justice under the Old Republic's rule for 25,000 years. But the Republic had been overthrown. Now the galaxy was ruled by the evil Galactic Empire.

The ruthless Emperor Palpatine had legions of soldiers and stormtroopers to command. The Imperial forces included gigantic Star Destroyers patrolling the galaxy and deadly TIE starfighters ready to fly into combat. There were even whispers that the Empire had developed a deadly superweapon powerful enough to shatter an entire planet.

Citizens of the Old Republic formed the Rebel Alliance to win back the rule of the galaxy. What followed was the long, fierce battle between the Rebels and the Imperials called the Galactic Civil War. News of the upstart Rebellion spread even to the distant Outer Rim Territories. In that star system was the desert world of Tatooine, where young Luke Skywalker lived on a moisture farm with his aunt and uncle. But Luke hadn't given his heart to the business of farming. Luke dreamed instead of the adventures awaiting him beyond the horizon. He dreamed of fighting for the Rebellion.

One day, Luke and his uncle purchased an astromech droid and a protocol droid from the roaming Jawa traders. Luke soon discovered that R2-D2 (the astromech droid) had a holographic message stored in its memory banks. The hologram was the image of a young woman wearing a white robe. She asked for Obi-Wan Kenobi's help. Could she mean Old Ben, the hermit who lived out by the desert wasteland known as the Dune Sea?

R2's impulse to deliver the message was so strong the little droid set out on its own to find Obi-Wan. Luke and C-3PO (the protocol droid) followed, joining up with R2 in the dangerous desert wasteland. Here Luke and C-3PO keep a lookout for the dangerous Tusken Raiders who roam these desert wastes.

When Luke and Ben finally met, the old hermit told young Skywalker that he was indeed the legendary Obi-Wan. As they all sat together in Obi-Wan's home, R2-D2 played the holographic message. The recorded image was of Princess Leia Organa, one of the leaders of the Rebellion. Leia begged Obi-Wan to join the fight against the Empire. She explained that hidden in R2 were plans vital to the survival of the Rebellion.

Obi-Wan (Ben) Kenobi's house in the Dune Sea.

Obi-Wan told Luke how he had fought for the Republic in the Clone Wars, the last great conflict before the Emperor rose to power. Then Obi-Wan revealed that Luke's father had been a Jedi Knight. He gave Luke his father's lightsaber, the prized weapon of a Jedi. And he told Luke about the Force. "The Force is what gives the Jedi his power. It's an energy field created by all living things. It surrounds us and penetrates us. It binds the galaxy together."

Obi-Wan asked Luke to join him in the Rebellion. At first, Luke said no—he was nervous about the sudden opportunity and knew he had responsibilities to his aunt and uncle. But while they were talking in Ben's home, tragedy struck at Luke's farm. In pursuit of the Imperial secrets stolen and hidden in R2-D2, the Empire staged a stormtrooper attack. Luke's uncle and aunt had been killed, their farm reduced to smoking ruins. When Luke learned this, he immediately decided to join Obi-Wan in the fight against the Empire. "I want to learn the ways of the Force and become a Jedi like my father," Luke told Obi-Wan. Luke Skywalker's destiny had begun to take shape.

I

THE REBEL
ORGANIZATION

The Rebel Alliance was vastly outnumbered by Imperial forces. The Rebels couldn't match the firepower of even a single Imperial Star Destroyer. To survive and have a chance to win the Civil War, the Rebellion would have to outsmart the Empire.

There were many courageous leaders in the Rebel forces. The Rebel leaders and their fighting troops were stationed at secret bases throughout the galaxy. There they waited for the signal to strike.

REBEL LEADERS

PRINCESS LEIA ORGANA

Leia, a Princess and Senator from her adopted home planet of Alderaan, was one of the great leaders of the Rebellion.

Leia risked her life to put the message for Obi-Wan into R2-D2's memory banks. Although Leia's ship had been captured by a Star Destroyer commanded by the feared Darth Vader, the droid had escaped to Tatooine. Leia's actions brought the Jedi Knight Obi-Wan Kenobi and young Luke Skywalker into the fight. But even more important were the secret plans stolen by the Rebels and hidden in R2-D2— the technical readouts of the dreaded Death Star, the Empire's ultimate weapon!

MON MOTHMA

As a respected, honorable Senator during the twilight of the Old Republic, Mon Mothma saw firsthand the growing decay and corruption of the ancient government. She witnessed Senator Palpatine's transformation from an ordinary politician to a ruthless Emperor. When Emperor Palpatine dissolved the Senate, Mon Mothma helped organize the underground Alliance to Restore the Republic. Her strategy was to organize small resistance factions throughout the galaxy and chip away at the Empire's strength with strategic battles.

ADMIRAL ACKBAR

Ackbar (pictured here in the center) was a senior advisor to Mon Mothma and a brilliant military strategist. Ackbar's people, who lived on the planet Mon Calamari, had always been peace-loving. But that didn't stop the Empire from invading Ackbar's homeworld. The destruction of many of Mon Calamari's great cities was meant to warn the entire galaxy not to oppose the Emperor's New Order. But the invasion only made the proud Mon Calamari species join the Rebellion, with Ackbar emerging as one of the great leaders of the resistance.

OBI-WAN (BEN) KENOBI

As a Jedi Knight, Obi-Wan was one of the last living links to the glory days of the Old Republic. He had been a general in the Clone Wars, the bloody conflict in which the Republic defeated the evil Mandalore warriors. When Darth Vader, the Emperor's personal dark knight, began tracking down and killing all the Jedi, Obi-Wan went into hiding in the wastelands of Tatooine.

Obi-Wan also knew a great secret—Darth Vader was actually Luke Skywalker and Princess Leia's father! Before Darth Vader became a symbol of the Empire's New Order, he had been known as Anakin Skywalker, a friend and student of Obi-Wan Kenobi. But while learning the ways of the Force, Anakin became attracted to the dark side. When Obi-Wan made one last attempt to turn his friend and pupil back to the light side, the two crossed lightsaber blades. During the battle Anakin fell into a molten pit. What emerged from the pit was a scorched shell of a man, full of hatred. In that dark moment, Anakin became Darth Vader, Dark Lord of the Sith.

Obi-Wan knew that as with Luke's father, the Force was strong with Luke. But the deadly lure of the dark side was always there. Obi-Wan feared what might happen when the time came for Luke to face his father.

LUKE SKYWALKER

Luke, the farm boy from Tatooine, would become a great Rebel leader and starfighter pilot. But Luke would also find himself on the path to becoming a true Jedi Knight. Both Obi-Wan and the Jedi Master Yoda would teach Luke self-control, to master the ancient art of the lightsaber, and to become one with the light side of the Force.

Here Luke has just arrived at Yoda's home on the planet Dagobah, where he has something to eat after his long voyage.

R2-D2

R2-D2 is an astromech droid, and specializes in spaceship repair, maintenance, and navigation.

When Princess Leia inserted the stolen Death Star plans in this little astromech droid, there was still the danger the secrets would be reclaimed by the Empire. After all, while Leia was hiding the plans in R2, her consular ship was being boarded by an Imperial force led by Darth Vader himself. But R2 had the intelligence to enter an escape pod of the ship (along with C-3PO). The pod fell away from the ship and landed on the nearby planet Tatooine. Later, loyal R2 would follow Luke Skywalker into battle as an assistant on board Luke's X-wing starfighter.

C-3PO

This golden protocol droid is fluent in over six million galactic languages and has recorded many of the great events of the Rebellion. C-3PO would follow Luke and Leia throughout some of the great battles and events of the Civil War. Although C-3PO is usually seen bickering with R2, the two droids are inseparable friends.

HAN SOLO

Known throughout the star systems as a great smuggler and superb pilot of his battle-ready freighter ship, the *Millennium Falcon*, Solo was one of many who didn't care whether the Old Republic or the Empire governed the galaxy. Or at least he didn't admit it.

But one day, while having a drink at the famed cantina in the spaceport town of Mos Eisley, Solo was approached by an old man and a young boy. The duo—Obi-Wan Kenobi and Luke Skywalker—wanted the fearless pilot to fly them off-planet. Han agreed, not realizing he was about to be pulled into the struggle against the Empire.

CHEWBACCA

Chewbacca, a Wookiee, serves Han as first mate and copilot on the *Millennium Falcon*. "Chewie" (as Solo affectionately calls him) is strong, brave, a great mechanic, and Han Solo's loyal friend. Later, Chewbacca would follow Han into the thick of the Rebel struggle. Here we see Chewie in a rare moment of recreation. On board the *Falcon*, he plays a hologame with C-3PO.

SECRET BASES

The Alliance's military strategy against the Empire was to strike quickly at specific targets. The Rebellion's underground movement was forced to plot and prepare its missions from secret bases. With the Empire constantly searching for these bases, the Rebels always had to be ready to evacuate. Generally, these secret bases were located on remote wilderness worlds.

YAVIN BASE

Yavin is a giant gaseous planet in the Yavin star system. The Alliance established one of its most successful bases on this planet's fourth moon. It was from the Yavin Base that the Alliance would launch one of its greatest victories.

Yavin 4 is covered with tropical jungle. Here a Rebel sentry keeps a watchful eye on the horizon. The *Millennium Falcon*, bearing Luke Skywalker, Princess Leia, Han Solo, Chewbacca, and the droids, has just flown into the Rebel airspace.

Dotted throughout Yavin's tropical woods are ancient pyramids and crumbling temples. They are the last remains of the lost Massassi, a mysterious civilization that once lived here. In a huge, deserted temple, the Rebels established their Yavin Base.

Pictured here is the Yavin hangar, where the Rebel pilots keep their X-wing and Y-wing starfighters ready for battle. In addition to the hangar and launch bay, this facility has a war room and command post, barracks, and storerooms.

ECHO BASE

While Yavin Base was set amid a wilderness world of tropical jungle, Echo Base was located in an ice cave on the freezing wastelands of the ice planet Hoth. The base was outfitted with huge doors that were kept closed at night to keep out the subzero temperatures. In total there were seven levels to house the Rebels' starfighters, snowspeeders, troops, briefing rooms, and equipment.

Here C-3PO and R2-D2 move through a chilly corridor on Echo Base.

An intense Leia in the Echo Base command center.

Hoth was selected as a Rebel base because of its location in a distant star system. The harsh conditions were so inhospitable that the Rebels hoped the Empire would never suspect they had established a base there. Death is always near in a world of freezing wind and temperatures, constant blizzards, snow, and ice.

The furry tauntauns are bipedal animals native to Hoth. The Rebels were able to domesticate some tauntauns, using them as pack animals or outfitting them with saddles for riding short distances. Here Luke Skywalker sits tall in the saddle.

The wampa ice creature is another animal native to Hoth. These giant animals are covered with white fur. They use their sharp claws to dig their lairs out of ice. With their razor-sharp teeth they tear at the flesh of their victims. Wampas store their prey in large ice caves. One horrible day Luke Skywalker himself was a wampa's prey....

Luke had ridden a tauntaun a short distance from Echo Base when he was attacked by a wampa. The ice creature dragged the unconscious Luke to its cave and hung him upside down from the ceiling. Luke awoke just in time to find himself prisoner in the wampa's cave. His lightsaber had fallen in the snow, just out of reach. But Luke had been training in the ways of the Force. With a mental burst of energy, Luke willed the weapon to fly up into his hand. Using the powerful lightsaber blade, Luke defended himself against the creature's attack.

MON CALAMARI STAR CRUISER

During the final stages of the Galactic Civil War, the Alliance leadership shifted from a secret land base to a mobile one. Under Admiral Ackbar's command, this spaceship served as Headquarters Frigate for the Alliance. Able to move through hyperspace and direct a Rebel assault, the cruiser served as both a battleship and command post.

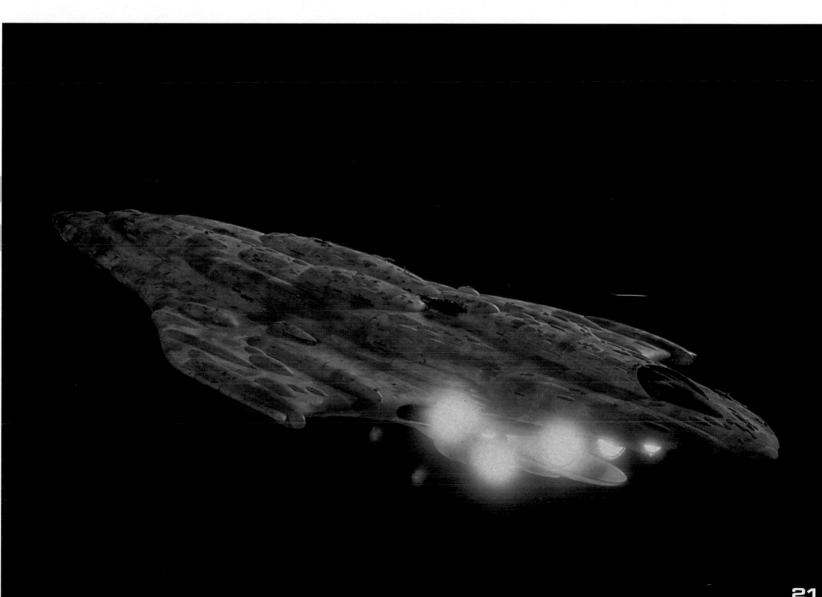

"Hokey religions and ancient weapons are no match for a good blaster at your side, kid," Han Solo once told Luke Skywalker. Luke was beginning to learn the ways of the Force from Obi-Wan Kenobi, much to Han's amusement. It was easy to see why Han was teasing the young Jedi-in-training. The Old Republic had been swept away. The Jedi Knights were a legend. The Force was considered mere superstition. And against the firepower of the Empire, it had been blasters and X-wing torpedo fire that had kept the Rebel cause alive.

But there was a reason Princess Leia had put great effort into drawing Obi-Wan into the struggle. Obi-Wan represented the noble tradition of the Jedi Knights. And only through the light side of the Force could the Rebellion hope to defeat the Empire.

Fate led to Obi-Wan and Luke Skywalker joining forces. It was during their first meeting in Obi-Wan's home that the Jedi Knight personally asked Luke to help revive the dying tradition. "You must learn the ways of the Force," the old master had told Luke. "I need your help, Luke. She [Princess Leia] needs your help."

Every journey begins with a first step. Here we see Obi-Wan and Luke in the *Millennium Falcon* as the Jedi Master gives Luke his first lessons in the ways of the Force.

SEEKER REMOTE

A great martial arts training tool, the seeker remote allows a Jedi student to practice lightsaber skills against a moving target. When in use, the floating seeker remote hovers in the air, ready to deliver stinging, nonlethal blasts. An antigravity device keeps the remote aloft. There are also military models that are equipped to shoot to kill.

WEAPONS OF WAR

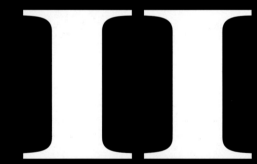

II

Since the Imperial forces vastly outnumbered the Rebel forces, the Alliance military strategy was to move fast, discover the Imperial Achilles' heel, and concentrate their firepower at that weak point. The Rebels did have a few giant combat starships, such as the Mon Calamari star cruiser commanded by Admiral Ackbar. But most of the Rebel arsenal was built for speed.

X-WING STARFIGHTERS

These single-pilot starfighters are made of double-layered wings. They are called "X" wings because, when in attack position, the wings separate to form an X shape. X-wing starfighters are fast, maneuverable, armed with four laser cannons, and equipped with defensive shields, hyperdrive, and other features.

One of the major features of the X-wing is a socket built into the hull behind the pilot's cockpit. Into this opening an astromech droid can be placed. (This opening has also been called a "droid interface socket.") The droid can then assist the pilot as a copilot, helping work the onboard computer, perform ship maintenance, and complete other functions. Here we see R2-D2 being lifted up into the astromech socket of Luke Skywalker's X-wing.

X-wing armada in combat formation.

Y-WING STARFIGHTERS

These twin-engine ships are an older version of the X-wing. Y-wing features include a hull socket for the droid interface, deflector shields, and two forward-mounted laser cannons. Here we see a Y-wing docked in Yavin Base hangar.

MILLENNIUM FALCON

Although not part of the regular Rebel armada, this ship played a key role in the Civil War. Once owned by Lando Calrissian, the *Falcon* was won from Lando by Han Solo in a gambling game. Although the *Falcon* was a light freighter (perfect for Solo's smuggling operations) Solo and Chewbacca improved the ship. The *Falcon* was outfitted with better deflector shields, a more powerful hyperdrive, and a weapons system.

Here the *Falcon* blasts off from Mos Eisley, barely escaping capture by Imperial stormtroopers.

Chewbacca, a master mechanic, busily working on the *Falcon* while it's docked in the Rebel Echo Base hangar.

Part of the *Falcon*'s weapons systems include turrets armed with laser cannons. During one space battle, Han and Luke each manned the controls of a laser cannon and defeated a group of attacking TIE fighters. Here we see Han in a turret at the controls of a laser cannon.

BLASTERS

Blasters—the weapons favored by Han Solo—fire intense light energy bolts. They can be set for stun or kill. Here we see Han Solo in action, firing away with his blaster at a group of stormtroopers.

LIGHTSABERS

While teaching Luke how to handle a lightsaber, Obi-Wan explained that the lightsaber was an "elegant weapon for a more civilized time." It was the great weapon of the glory era of the Old Republic. While a blaster simply requires aiming and squeezing the trigger, using a lightsaber takes a great deal of skill and practice.

The lightsaber itself is a small handle, which serves as the handgrip. Inside are power cells and crystals that, when activated, generate a three- to four-foot-long blade of pure energy. This blade can cut through almost any object, except another lightsaber beam.

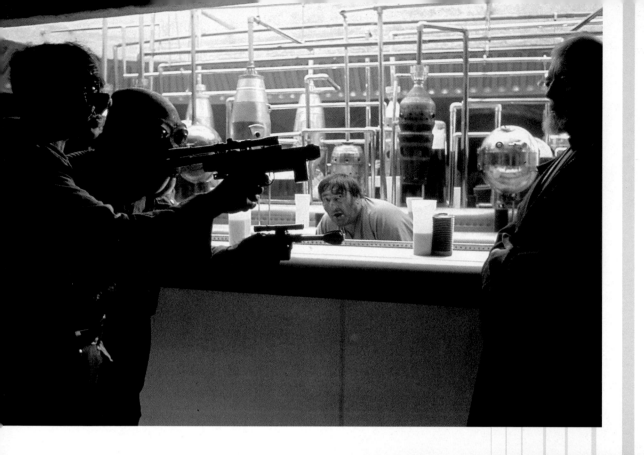

In the rough-and-tough Mos Eisley Cantina, Luke Skywalker was threatened by a ruffian named Dr. Evazan. Obi-Wan came to Luke's aid, and Dr. Evazan pulled out his blaster. But the blaster was no match for the lightsaber of a Jedi Knight.

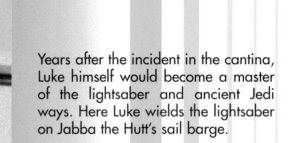

Years after the incident in the cantina, Luke himself would become a master of the lightsaber and ancient Jedi ways. Here Luke wields the lightsaber on Jabba the Hutt's sail barge.

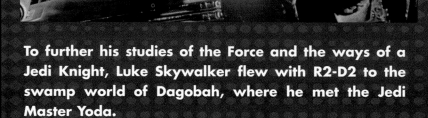

To further his studies of the Force and the ways of a Jedi Knight, Luke Skywalker flew with R2-D2 to the swamp world of Dagobah, where he met the Jedi Master Yoda.

One of the goals of great cultures is to train both mind and body. So it is with students of the Jedi path. Here Yoda puts Luke through a tough workout that would make him both healthy and physically strong.

The philosophy of the Jedi Knight is to clear the mind of questions. It's also important not to make excuses, but to take personal responsibility for one's actions. One of Yoda's famous sayings is: "Do. Or do not. There is no try."

A Jedi Knight's strength flows from the Force. This power can even enable one to perform supernatural feats. But such power means nothing without a pure heart. Arrogance and self-pride come when one is in the pull of the dark side of the Force. That dark path is the way of anger, fear, and aggression.

Even though Darth Vader killed Obi-Wan in battle, the great Jedi Knight was still able to communicate with Luke through the Force. Here Obi-Wan's spirit talks with Luke. Among the secrets confirmed are that Vader is Luke's own father, and Leia his long-lost twin sister!

III

THE FIGHTING FORCE

While Rebel leaders such as Mon Mothma, Admiral Ackbar, and Princess Leia planned the battle strategy, it was the starfighter pilots and foot soldiers who ultimately put the plans into action.

ROGUE SQUADRON

The X-wing squadron that attacked the first Death Star later became known as Rogue Squadron. This famous group included Luke Skywalker, Luke's childhood friend Biggs Darklighter, and Wedge Antilles. Sadly, Biggs was killed in the Battle of Yavin. But the squadron went on to perform heroically in the battle of Yavin.

Here are photo portraits of some of the great starfighter pilots of the Galactic Civil War.

Biggs Darklighter.

Wedge Antilles.

Zev Senesca.

Dack Ralter.

HAN SOLO

In addition to the squadron leaders, there were some heroic rogue pilots, notably Han Solo and Lando Calrissian.

Although Solo had been a smuggler who seemed to care only for money, he was a brave man with a good heart. It was while piloting Obi-Wan and Luke that he began to witness the evil acts of the Empire.

Han began to prove himself by helping Luke rescue Princess Leia from the first Death Star. He would soon become friends with Luke, and would even fall in love with Leia (and she with him!).

Han survived being captured by Vader and frozen in carbonite (with Luke and Leia leading Han's rescue from the fortress prison of Jabba's palace on Tatooine). And Han would play a key role in the final battle between Alliance and Empire.

Here we see some of Han's fancy flying as he dodges Imperial starfighters (above) and makes his way around dangerous asteroid fields (below).

LANDO CALRISSIAN

Lando Calrissian, another one-time rogue and gambler, would join in the Rebel fight, too. In the Battle of Endor, he would get the chance to pilot his old ship, the *Millennium Falcon*. Here we see Lando during his time as Baron Administrator of the floating Cloud City above Bespin.

Lando was at the controls of the *Falcon* during a daring rescue of Luke Skywalker. Luke had been defeated in battle by Vader and had fallen through the Cloud City reactor shaft. Clinging to a weather vane at the bottom of the city, Luke had mentally called out to Leia for help. The Princess heard Luke's voice and instructed Lando to turn the *Falcon* back to save the fallen warrior. Later Lando would be made general and would lead the attack on the second Death Star.

Nien Nunb, Sullastan copilot for Lando Calrissian. Nunb was in the cockpit with Lando when he commanded the *Millennium Falcon* as the lead starfighter in the attack on the second Death Star.

We have seen the leaders and famous faces of the Rebel Alliance. But the success of the Rebellion depended on the help of millions and millions throughout the star systems.

FOOT SOLDIERS

Rebel foot soldiers on Hoth. Many brave soldiers would give their lives when the Imperial forces, led by Darth Vader, invaded the Rebel Echo Base.

EWOKS

The Ewoks of Endor's forest moon (also known as the "Sanctuary Moon") are a good example of a people being drawn into the Rebel cause. The Empire had taken over their world in order to build a shield generator that would protect the second Death Star while under construction. The Empire felt the primitive, furry, forest-dwelling Ewoks would pose no threat. But the Ewoks would play a key role in the last major battle of the Civil War.

Two views of an Ewok village nestled among the moon's gigantic forests.

Glimpses of Ewok warriors.

When C-3PO travels to the Sanctuary Moon, the Ewoks worship the glittering gold droid as a god!

The galaxy is full of miraculous sights. It is filled with star systems, planets, and varied species. It is a universe worth saving. Here are some glimpses of the depths of space.

Cloud City, in the clouds above the gas planet Bespin.

Tatooine, with its twin suns and vast deserts, is a planet of heat and sand. Here Luke, out for a ride in his landspeeder, surveys a flat stretch of desert.

On planet Tatooine, near the Dune Sea, is the region known as the Jundland Wastes. Here C-3PO passes the skeletal remains of the krayt dragons that live in the surrounding mountains.

Hoth, with its ice, snow, and freezing temperatures, is a world of endless cold.

REBEL TRIUMPHS

Although the Galactic Civil War raged for years, several key battles would decide the conflict. Two of the great Alliance victories were centered around different Imperial Death Star battle stations. The Death Star was the Empire's ultimate weapon. It was as big as a small moon. A Death Star could hold more than 7,000 TIE fighters and more than a million combat troops. But most horrifying of all was the Death Star superlaser, which could destroy an entire planet.

Massed against this great power were squadrons of X-wing starfighters, fearless pilots, and battle plans prepared by the Rebel leaders.

The power of the first Death Star was awesome and terrible as demonstrated with the destruction of the peaceful planet Alderaan. Thankfully, the Death Star plans stolen by the Rebel Alliance revealed a weakness in the battle station. A long trench on the battle station's surface had an open exhaust vent. The vent led directly down into the reactor core of the station. A direct hit from an X-wing proton torpedo could cause a chain reaction that would explode the Death Star.

Unfortunately, the vent was only six feet wide. It would take a miracle shot to hit the target. But the Rebels had no choice but to try. The Empire had already located the Rebel's secret base on Yavin 4. As the Rebel pilots and starfighters prepared for the Death Star attack, the dread battle station moved within range of Yavin. When close enough, the Death Star laser would easily be able to destroy the Rebel base . . . and the entire world.

The Rebel squadrons blast off from Yavin base.
Next stop: the Death Star.

The attacking X-wings are met by Imperial TIE fighters.

A TIE downs a Rebel starfighter.

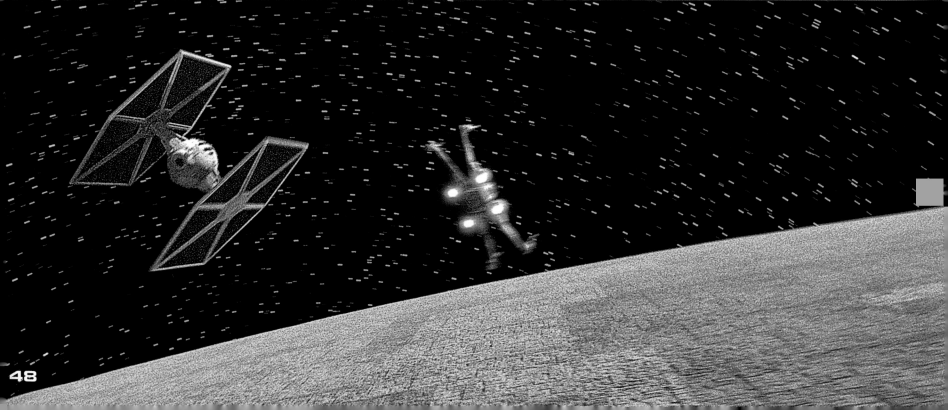

Another Rebel starfighter—destroyed!

One of the Rebel star pilots makes it through the trench. The pilot fires a torpedo at the target. It misses! Now it is up to Luke to attempt one final shot. But Imperial combat ships led by Darth Vader's TIE interceptor follow Luke down the trench.

R2-D2 is hit by TIE fighter fire.

As Luke flies closer to his target, he hears the voice of Obi-Wan Kenobi. "Use the Force, Luke," says Obi-Wan. "Trust me." Luke concentrates, letting the Force flow through him. But Darth Vader is hot on his tail. Just when it seems that Darth Vader is about to blast Luke's X-wing, the *Millennium Falcon* comes to the rescue. Han's blast allows his friend time to attempt the final shot. "You're all clear, kid," Han shouts over the radio. "Now let's blow this thing and go home!"

Han's blast from the *Falcon* knocks a TIE into Vader's ship, which flies into space. The TIE then explodes in the trench.

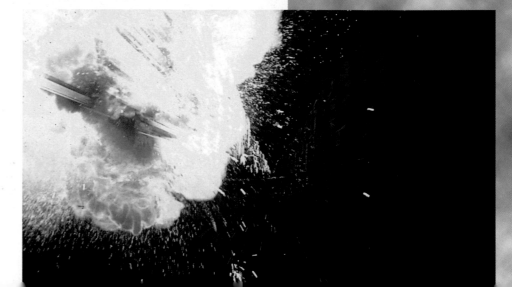

Luke's mind is now clear of confusion. He releases the torpedoes…and makes a direct hit! As Luke flies to safety, the chain reaction builds and the Death Star explodes.

Rebel celebration, Yavin Base throne room.

After the destruction of the Death Star, there was great celebration. Princess Leia herself gave medals to three of the battle's greatest heroes: Luke, Han, and Chewbacca. But the Rebels knew that though they'd won the battle, they hadn't won the war. The Imperial forces would quickly regroup. The Emperor could order the construction of a bigger Death Star. And now that the location of Yavin Base was known to the Empire, the Rebels would have to find another home. Still, the Rebels had won a great victory. For the moment, at least, they could rejoice.

After the triumph of Yavin, the Rebels set up a new secret base on the ice planet Hoth. But the Empire soon discovered the location and invaded. The resulting Battle of Hoth was one of the worst defeats for the Rebellion. Just as the Empire had regrouped after the Battle of Yavin, the Rebels now found themselves having to regroup.

The Battle of Endor would decide the entire Civil War. The Emperor had arrived at the new Death Star, which was under construc-tion. From his Death Star throne room, the evil Emperor would oversee what he believed would be the final battle, and the end of the Rebellion.

For the Rebels it was another race against time. Even though the new Death Star was still under construction, its new superlaser was almost operational. Once completed, this ultimate battle station would make the Empire virtually invincible.

The Rebel leaders directed the battle from space. It would be an attack on two fronts. A group led by Han Solo would try to destroy the protective shield generator on the forest moon. Then a squadron led by Lando Calrissian would be able to fly directly into the battle station, and fire on the main reactor, blowing it up. Here we see Lando, Chewie, Han, and Leia listening during the briefing in the Mon Calamari cruiser.

On Endor, an Imperial trap awaited Han and his team.

But the Empire's stormtroopers hadn't expected the primitive Ewoks to join the Rebels in their fight.

With the Ewoks fighting alongside the Rebels, the Death Star shield generator was destroyed. Without the invisible protective shield around the Death Star, General Lando Calrissian and copilot Nien Nunb flew into the battle station. After firing the blasts that set off the chain reaction, Lando piloted the *Falcon* to safety just moments before the huge Death Star explosion.

THE BATTLES OF LUKE SKYWALKER

The Battle of Endor was fought on land and in space. But there was another battlefront—the Death Star throne room. There Luke Skywalker finally confronted both the Emperor and Darth Vader.

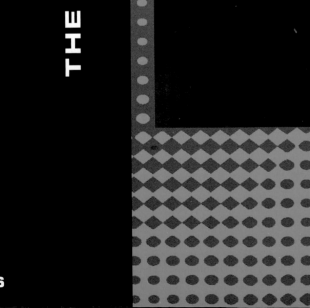

THE BATTLE AT THE SARLACC PIT

The last time Luke had faced Vader in Cloud City, the Dark Lord had defeated him. But Luke had not yet become one with the Force. Since that dark day in Cloud City, Luke had developed his self-control and discipline. Luke had learned a lot. He had grown up.

THRONE ROOM ON THE SECOND DEATH STAR

In the throne room battle against Vader, Luke showed that he had attained the spiritual compassion of a true Jedi Knight. He fought Vader in self-defense, and when he defeated Vader, he refused to kill him. He saw not the masked and armored Vader but the man who was his father. He believed the noble heart of the Jedi Anakin Skywalker still lived underneath Vader's black suit of armor.

The Emperor smiled at the sight of Luke mastering Vader in combat. He urged Luke to kill Vader and give himself to the dark side. But Luke refused. "Never!" he exclaimed. "I'll never turn to the dark side. You've failed, Your Highness. I am a Jedi, like my father before me."

The Emperor's evil smile turned to a frown. Suddenly, deadly bolts of energy shot out from the Emperor's fingertips. As Luke fell to the ground in pain, he called out to his father for help.

For years Vader had called the Emperor "Master." But Luke had awakened the sleeping soul of Anakin Skywalker. With his last bit of strength, the Dark Lord picked up the Emperor and threw him down a shaft to his death. As the man known as Vader collapsed, Luke removed his black helmet. After so many years, so many battles, father and son could look into each other's eyes at last.

Though Anakin died, Luke carried his body onto a shuttle and blasted off just before the Death Star exploded. On the Sanctuary Moon of Endor, Luke laid his father's body on a funeral pyre. Luke was sad but felt some comfort. Darth Vader, master of the dark side, had died in the Emperor's throne room. Anakin Skywalker, loving father and Jedi Knight, had been reborn.

EPILOGUE: CELEBRATION

With the destruction of the second Death Star, the end of Vader, and the death of the Emperor, the long Galactic Civil War was over. The Rebellion had won! Throughout the galaxy, on all the different worlds, celebrations were held.

Crowds fill the streets of Mos Eisley, on the planet Tatooine.

Fireworks explode across the sky above Endor as the Ewoks and
the Rebels celebrate their victory over the Galactic Empire.

On the forest moon of Endor, the Rebel heroes gather with the Ewoks.

Luke Skywalker's heart filled with joy during the celebration in the Ewok village. And not just because of the great Rebel victory. Standing there, shimmering with light, were three friendly figures: Obi-Wan, Yoda, and his father, Anakin. The three great Jedi had smiles on their faces as they watched the celebration. Their smiles seemed to offer a promise to Luke, the young Jedi Knight. "The Force will be with you—always!"

Author's Credits

Mark Cotta Vaz has written two other books in this Star Wars Trilogy Scrapbook series: *The Complete Star Wars Trilogy Scrapbook* and *The Galactic Empire Scrapbook*. His other Lucasfilm books include *Secrets of Star Wars: Shadows of the Empire* and *From Star Wars to Indiana Jones: The Best of the Lucasfilm Archives* (with Shinji Hata).